The Winter J

The Winter Journey

GEORGES PEREC

Translated by JOHN STURROCK

SYRENS

GEORGES PEREC 1936–1982

S Y R E N S Published by the Penguin Group. Penguin Books Ltd, 27 Wrights
Lane, London w8 5tz, England. Penguin Books USA Inc., 375 Hudson Street, New
York, New York 10014, USA. Penguin Books Australia Ltd, Ringwood, Victoria,
Australia. Penguin Books Canada Ltd, 10 Alcorn Avenue, Toronto, Ontario, Canada
m4v 3b2. Penguin Books (NZ) Ltd, 182–190 Wairau Road, Auckland 10, New
Zealand. Penguin Books Ltd, Registered Offices: Harmondsworth, Middlesex, Eng-
land. First published by Les Éditions du Seuil 1993. Published in Syrens 1995.
Copyright © Les Éditions du Seuil, 1993. Translation copyright © John Sturrock,
1995. All rights reserved. The moral right of the author has been asserted. Except in the
United States of America, this book is sold subject to the condition that it shall not, by
way of trade or otherwise, be lent, re-sold, hired out, or otherwise circulated without
the publisher's prior consent in any form of binding or cover other than that in which
it is published and without a similar condition including this condition being imposed
on the subsequent purchaser. Set in 12.5/16pt Monotype Bembo by Datix International
Limited, Bungay, Suffolk. Printed and bound by Page Bros., Norwich.

Famous he may have become, as an unimaginably skilful and much enjoyed player of literary games, but Georges Perec still wouldn't put himself forward as a writer. *The Winter Journey* appeared for a first time in 1980, secretly almost, in a publicity bulletin put out by the Paris house of Hachette. Three years later, soon after Perec's too early death (at 46), it was rescued from that PR person's oubliette, to appear for a second time in a literary paper. Ten years after that, it was re-rescued and appeared definitively in a volume of its own: a delightful, very Perecquian small fiction more than fit to keep no company but its own. This indeed could be mistaken for a story by the absolute master of such sly literary fancies, Jorge Luis Borges. It is based on a single, delicate, inspired thought, which would be wonderfully upsetting of received literary ideas were it only able to be realized. It begins in a library and ends in an asylum, a whimsical trajectory of the sort the unfailingly modest Perec liked.

The literature that the story draws on is necessarily French, but that needn't hold anyone back from taking pleasure in what Perec gets up to here. No great knowledge – no knowledge at all perhaps – of French literature is needed in order to appreciate it: the names of the poets and the lines he quotes from them could all be changed from French to English, without in any way spoiling the point of the joke. Some of the versifiers that Perec cites are the great names of the *fin de siècle* – Mallarmé, Rimbaud, Verlaine – others are the obscurest of the obscure, forgotten no-hopers. The grandest name of all is that of Victor Hugo, the supreme French poet of the nineteenth century, whose initials mirror – by that I mean reverse – those of Perec's startlingly anticipatory poet, Hugo Vernier: the shared Hugo, family name in one case, given name in the other, is the source of confusions that are of value to Perec's plot. Names always help to explain things when this ultra-methodical writer is at work, and the names in *The Winter Journey* drop some useful hints. Vernier, for one: look it up in an (English) dictionary and you'll find that a vernier (named for its French inventor) is a small scale enabling one to adjust a larger scale to give fractional readings, which is something like the mirror image (again) of what Hugo Vernier's 'brief œuvre' achieves in the story. Then there's the name of Perec's obsessed hero, Vincent Degraël: given his quest, and his ironic fate, it's surely allowable to see and to hear in his surname the word Grail – and the name Vincent, let's not forget, means 'conquering'.

Along with the names, the dates also are worth attending to in *The Winter Journey*, because they are less casual than they seem. September 3, the date of Vernier's supposed birth, was also the day on which the Second World War began; and 1836, the year of his birth, was a hundred years exactly before Perec's own year of birth. Connections seem suddenly to be forming between Vernier, Perec and the 1939–45 war. That is an event passed through quickly, safely – almost magically – by Degraël, who survives to resume his researches after it has ended. It was not an event survived so easily by Perec himself, a young Jewish boy whose soldier father died of his wounds in June 1940, and whose mother was deported to a death camp from which she did not come back. Degraël survives the war, but the evidence of his astounding discovery does not: it is the war that has derailed him. Even in a story as carefree and timeless on the face of things as *The Winter Journey*, details are so arranged as to remind us that Georges Perec was something more than the frivolous writer he might seem to be.

The Winter Journey

In the last week of August 1939, as the talk of war invaded Paris, a young literature teacher, Vincent Degraël, was invited to spend a few days at the place outside Le Havre belonging to the parents of one of his colleagues, Denis Borrade. The day before his departure, while exploring his hosts' shelves in search of one of those books one has always promised oneself one will read, but that one will generally only have time to leaf inattentively through beside the fire before going to make up a fourth at bridge, Degraël lit upon a slim volume entitled *The Winter Journey*, whose author, Hugo Vernier, was quite unknown to him but whose opening pages made so strong an impression on him that he barely found time to make his excuses to his friend and his parents before going up to his room to read it.

The Winter Journey was a sort of narrative written in the first person, and set in a semi-imaginary country whose heavy skies, gloomy forests, mild hills and canals interrupted by greenish locks evoked with an insidious insistence the landscapes of Flanders and the Ardennes. The book was divided into two parts.

The first, shorter part retraced in sibylline terms a journey which had all the appearances of an initiation, whose every stage seemed certainly to have been marked by a failure, and at the end of which the anonymous hero, a man whom everything gave one to suppose was young, arrived beside a lake that was submerged in a thick mist; there, a ferryman was waiting for him, who took him to a steep-sided, small island in the middle of which there rose a tall, gloomy building; hardly had the young man set foot on the narrow landing-stage that afforded the only access to the island when a strange-looking couple appeared: an old man and an old woman, both clad in long black capes, who seemed to rise up out of the fog and who came and placed themselves on either side of him, took hold of him by the elbows and pressed themselves as tightly as possible against his sides; welded together almost, they scaled a rock-strewn path, entered the house, climbed a wooden staircase and came to a bedroom. There, as inexplicably as they had appeared, the old people vanished, leaving the young man alone in the middle of the room. It was perfunctorily furnished: a bed covered with a flowery cretonne, a table, a chair. A fire was blazing in the fireplace. On the table a meal had been laid: bean soup, a shoulder of beef. Through the tall window of the room, the young man watched the full moon emerging from the clouds; then he sat down at the table and began to eat. This solitary supper brought the first part to an end.

The second part alone formed nearly four-fifths of the book and it quickly appeared that the brief narrative preceding it was merely an anecdotal pretext. It was a long confession of an exacerbated lyricism, mixed in with poems, with enigmatic maxims, with blasphemous incantations. Hardly had he begun reading it before Vincent Degraël felt a sense of unease that he found it impossible to define exactly, but which only grew more pronounced as he turned the pages of the volume with an increasingly shaky hand; it was as if the phrases he had in front of him had become suddenly familiar, were starting irresistibly to remind him of *something*, as if onto each one that he read there had been imposed, or rather superimposed, the at once precise yet blurred memory of a phrase almost identical to it that he had perhaps already read somewhere else; as if these words, more tender than a caress or more treacherous than a poison, words that were alternately limpid and hermetic, obscene and cordial, dazzling, labyrinthine, endlessly swinging like the frantic needle of a compass between a hallucinated violence and a fabulous serenity, formed the outline of a vague configuration in which could be found, jumbled together, Germain Nouveau and Tristan Corbière, Rimbaud and Verhaeren, Charles Cros and Léon Bloy.

These were the very authors with

whom Vincent Degraël was concerned
– for several years he had been working
on a thesis on the 'evolution of French
poetry from the Parnassians to the Sym-
bolists' – and his first thought was that
he might well have chanced to read
this book as part of his researches, then,
more likely, that he was the victim of
an illusory *déjà vu* in which, as when the
simple taste of a sip of tea suddenly
carries you back thirty years to England,
a mere trifle had sufficed, a sound, a
smell, a gesture – perhaps the moment's
hesitation he had noticed before taking
the book from the shelf where it had
been arranged between Verhaeren and
Vielé-Griffin, or else the eager way in
which he had perused the opening pages
– for the false memory of a previous

reading to superimpose itself and so to disturb his present reading as to make it impossible. Soon, however, doubt was no longer possible and Degraël had to yield to the evidence: perhaps his memory was playing tricks on him, perhaps it was only by chance that Vernier seemed to have borrowed his 'solitary jackal haunting stone sepulchres' from Catulle Mendès, perhaps it should be put down to a fortuitous convergence, to a parading of influence, a deliberate homage, unconscious copying, wilful pastiche, a liking for quotation, a fortunate coincidence, perhaps expressions such as 'the flight of time', 'winter fogs', 'dim horizon', 'deep caves', 'vaporous fountains', 'uncertain light of the wild undergrowth' should be seen as belonging by right to all poets so that it was just as normal to meet with them in a paragraph by Hugo Vernier as in the stanzas of Jean Moréas, but it was quite impossible not to recognize, word for word, or almost, reading at random, in one place a fragment from Rimbaud ('I readily could see a mosque in place of a factory, a drum school built by angels') or Mallarmé ('the lucid winter, the season of serene art'), in another Lautréamont ('I gazed in a mirror at that mouth bruised of my own volition'), Gustave Kahn ('Let the song expire ... my heart weeps/ A bistre crawls around the brightness/ The solemn silence has risen slowly, it frightens/ The familiar sounds of the shadowy staff') or, only slightly modified, Verlaine ('in the interminable

tedium of the plain, the snow gleamed
like sand. The sky was the colour of
copper. The train slid without a mur-
mur . . .') etc.

It was four o'clock in the morning
when Degraël finished reading *The
Winter Journey*. He had pinpointed some
thirty borrowings. There were certainly
others. Hugo Vernier's book seemed to
be nothing more than a prodigious com-
pilation from the poets of the end of the
nineteenth century, a disproportionate
cento, a mosaic almost every piece of
which was the work of someone else.
But at the same time as he was strug-
gling to imagine this unknown author
who had wanted to extract the very
matter of his own text from the books
of others, when he was attempting to

picture this admirable and senseless project to himself in its entirety, Degraël felt a wild suspicion arise in him: he had just remembered that in taking the book from the shelf he had automatically made a note of the date, impelled by that reflex of the young researcher who never consults a work without remarking the bibliographical details. Perhaps he had made a mistake, but he certainly thought he had read 1864. He checked it, his heart pounding. He had read it correctly: that would mean Vernier had 'quoted' a line of Mallarmé two years in advance, had plagiarized Verlaine ten years before his 'Forgotten ariettas', had written some Gustave Kahn nearly a quarter of a century before Kahn did! It would mean that Lautréamont, Germain

Nouveau, Rimbaud, Corbière and quite a few others were merely the copyists of an unrecognized poet of genius who, in a single work, had been able to bring together the very substance off which three or four generations would be feeding after him!

Unless, obviously, the printer's date that appeared on the book were wrong. But Degraël refused to entertain that hypothesis: his discovery was too beautiful, too obvious, too necessary not to be true, and he was already imagining the vertiginous consequences it would provoke: the prodigious scandal that the public revelation of this 'premonitory anthology' would occasion, the extent of the fallout, the enormous doubt that would be cast on all that the critics and literary historians had been imperturbably teaching for years and years. Such was his impatience that, abandoning sleep once and for all, he dashed down to the library to try and find out a little more about this Vernier and his work.

He found nothing. The few dictionaries and directories to be found in the Borrades' library knew nothing of the existence of Hugo Vernier. Neither Denis nor his parents were able to tell him anything further: the book had been bought at an auction, ten years before, in Honfleur; they had looked through it without paying it much attention.

All through the day, with Denis's help, Degraël proceeded to make a systematic examination of the book, going to look up its splintered fragments in dozens of anthologies and collections. They found almost three hundred and fifty, shared among almost thirty authors; the most celebrated along with the most obscure poets of the *fin de siècle*, and sometimes even a few prose writers (Léon Bloy, Ernest Hello), seemed to have used *The Winter Journey* as a bible from which they had extracted the best of themselves: Banville, Richepin, Huysmans, Charles Cros, Léon Valade rubbed shoulders with Mallarmé and Verlaine and others now fallen into oblivion whose names were Charles de Pomairols, Hippolyte Vaillant, Maurice Rollinat (the son-in-law of George Sand), Laprade, Albert Mérat, Charles Morice or Antony Valabrègue.

Degraël made a careful note of the

list of authors and the source of their borrowings and returned to Paris, fully determined to continue his researches the very next day in the Bibliothèque Nationale. But events did not allow him to. In Paris his call-up papers were waiting for him. Joining his unit in Compiègne, he found himself, without really having had the time to understand why, in Saint-Jean-de-Luz, passed over into Spain and from there to England, and only came back to France at the end of 1945. Throughout the war he had carried his notebook with him and had miraculously succeeded in not losing it. His researches had obviously not progressed much, but he had made one, for him capital, discovery all the same: in the British Museum he had been able to consult the *Catalogue général de la librairie française* and the *Bibliographie de la France* and been able to confirm his tremendous hypothesis: *The Winter Journey*, by Vernier (Hugo), had indeed been published in 1864, at Valenciennes, by Hervé Frères, Publishers and Booksellers, had been registered legally like all the books published in France, and had been deposited in the Bibliothèque Nationale, where it had been given the shelfmark z87912.

Appointed to a teaching post in Beauvais, Vincent Degraël henceforth devoted all his free time to *The Winter Journey*.

Going thoroughly into the private journals and correspondence of most of the poets of the end of the nineteenth century quickly convinced him that, in his day, Hugo Vernier had known the celebrity he deserved: notes such as 'received a letter from Hugo today', or 'wrote a long letter to Hugo', 'read V.H. all night', or even Valentin Havercamp's celebrated 'Hugo, Hugo alone' definitely did not refer to 'Victor' Hugo, but to this doomed poet whose brief œuvre had apparently inflamed all those who had held it in their hands. Glaring contradictions which criticism and literary history had never been able to explain thus found their one logical solution: it was obviously with Hugo Vernier in mind and what they owed to his *Winter Journey* that Rimbaud had written 'I is another', and Lautréamont 'Poetry should be made by all and not by one.'

But the more he established the preponderant place that Hugo Vernier was going to have to occupy in the literary history of late nineteenth-century France, the less was he in a position to furnish tangible proof: for he was never able to lay his hands again on a copy of *The Winter Journey*. The one he had consulted had been destroyed – along with the villa – during the bombing of Le Havre; the copy deposited in the Bibliothèque Nationale wasn't there when he asked for it and it was only after long inquiries that he was able to learn that, in 1926, the book had been sent to a binder who had never received it. All the researches that he caused to be undertaken by dozens, by hundreds of librarians, archivists and booksellers proved fruitless, and Degraël soon persuaded himself that the edition of five hundred copies had been deliberately destroyed by the very people who had been so directly inspired by it.

Of Hugo Vernier's life, Vincent Degraël learnt nothing, or next to nothing. An unlooked-for brief mention, unearthed in an obscure *Biographie des hommes remarquables de la France du Nord et de la Belgique* (Verviers, 1882), informed him that he had been born in Vimy (Pas-de-Calais) on 3 September 1836. But the records of the Vimy registry office had been burned in 1916, along with the duplicate copies lodged in the prefecture in Arras. No death certificate seemed ever to have been made out.

For close on thirty years, Vincent Degraël strove in vain to assemble proof of the existence of this poet and of his work. When he died, in the psychiatric hospital in Verrières, a few of his former pupils undertook to sort the vast pile of documents and manuscripts he had left behind. Among them figured a thick register bound in black cloth whose label bore, carefully and ornamentally inscribed, *The Winter Journey*. The first eight pages retraced the history of his fruitless researches; the 392 other pages were blank.

The Winter Journey (*Le Voyage d'hiver*) first appeared in a publisher's publicity bulletin, *Hachette Informations*, no. 18, March–April 1980. It was published in *Magazine littéraire*, no. 193, March 1983, a special edition devoted to Georges Perec. It was published in book form in October 1993 by Les Éditions du Seuil.